Date: 7/17/17

J GRA 741.5 SEE V.2
Seifert, Brandon,
Seekers of the weird.

SEEKERS OF THE WEIRD #2

MAXWELL and MELODY KEEP always thought their parents ARTHUR and ELLEN were weird, but nothing could have prepared them for the day their curio store was attacked by taxidermy monsters.

Aided by the sudden appearance of their estranged UNCLE ROLAND, Maxwell and Melody emerged unscathed, but their parents were abducted. A mysterious CANDLEMAN was left in their place, carrying a fiery message from DESPOINA of the SHADOW SOCIETY: deliver the COFFIN CLOCK before the Candleman burns down, or never see Arthur and Ellen again!

The teens followed Roland through a magical doorway in their burning home into the MUSEUM OF THE WEIRD, a place of moving statues and wondrous exhibits. Roland left, vowing to save the elder Keeps himself...only to return with his legs missing below the knee! He passed out from the magical wounds, leaving Maxwell and Melody alone in the bizarre museum!

BRANDON SEIFERT writer
KARL MOLINE penciler (1-14 & 20/layout artist 15-19)
RICK MAGYAR inker (1-14 & 20/finisher 15-19)
JEAN-FRANCOIS BEAULIEU colorist   VC'S JOE CARAMAGNA letterer

MICHAEL DEL MUNDO cover artist
BRIAN CROSBY & PASCAL CAMPION variant cover artists

JIM CLARK, BRIAN CROSBY, TOM MORRIS
& JOSH SHIPLEY walt disney imagineers

MARK BASSO assistant editor   BILL ROSEMANN editor

AXEL ALONSO editor in chief   JOE QUESADA chief creative officer
DAN BUCKLEY publisher

special thanks to DAVID GABRIEL

MUSEUM OF THE WEIRD inspired by the designs of ROLLY CRUMP

marvelkids.com

ABDOPUBLISHING.COM

Reinforced library bound edition published in 2017 by Spotlight,
a division of ABDO, PO Box 398166, Minneapolis, Minnesota 55439.
Spotlight produces high-quality reinforced library bound editions for
schools and libraries. Published by agreement with Marvel Characters, Inc.

Printed in the United States of America, North Mankato, Minnesota.
042016
092016

THIS BOOK CONTAINS
RECYCLED MATERIALS

marvelkids.com
© 2014 MARVEL

Elements based on
Walt Disney's
Museum of the Weird
© Disney.

PUBLISHER'S CATALOGING IN PUBLICATION DATA

Names: Seifert, Brandon, author. | Moline, Karl ; Magyar, Rick ; Beaulieu, Jean-Francois ;
    Andrade, Filipe, illustrators.
Title: Disney Kingdoms : Seekers of the weird / by Brandon Seifert ; illustrated by Karl Moline,
    Rick Magyar, Jean-Francois Beaulieu, and Filipe Andrade.
Description: Minneapolis, MN : Spotlight, [2017] | Series: Disney Kingdoms : seekers of the
    weird
Summary: When their parents are abducted, Melody and Maxwell Keep follow their estranged
    uncle Roland through a portal to the Museum of the Weird, and are thrust into a dangerous
    mission to save their family and the world from an evil shadow society!
Identifiers: LCCN 2016932365 | ISBN 9781614795148 (v.1 : lib. bdg.) | ISBN 9781614795155
    (v. 2 : lib. bdg.) | ISBN 9781614795162 (v. 3 : lib. bdg.) | ISBN 9781614795179 (v. 4 : lib.
    bdg.) | ISBN 9781614795186 (v. 5 : lib. bdg.)
Subjects: LCSH: Disney (Fictitious characters)--Juvenile fiction. | Rescues--Juvenile fiction. |
    Museums--Juvenile fiction. | Adventure and adventurers--Juvenile fiction. | Comic books,
    strips, etc.--Juvenile fiction. | Graphic novels--Juvenile fiction.
Classification: DDC 741.5--dc23
LC record available at http://lccn.loc.gov/2016932365

ABDO

Spotlight

A Division of ABDO
abdopublishing.com

I WISH WE'D WAKE UP.

IN OUR BEDS--

--IN OUR HOUSE, WHICH HADN'T ACTUALLY BURNED TO THE GROUND...

...WITH MOM AND DAD, WHO DIDN'T ACTUALLY GET KIDNAPPED BY MONSTERS.

I WISH UNCLE ROLAND WOULD WAKE UP ALREADY.

OH, FORGET THIS!

UH... MELODY?

WHERE ARE YOU GOING?

WHERE DO YOU THINK, MAXWELL?

I DON'T CARE IF IT'S BURNT TO THE GROUND. I DON'T CARE IF IT'S EVEN STILL ACTIVELY ON FIRE...

...I'M GOING HOME.

MELODY! DON'T OPEN THAT--

--SPIDER!

YOU *THREW A SPIDER* AT ME!

YES-- A *GRAPNEL SPIDER!* TO SAVE YOU!

HURRY, GRAB THE--

--WHEW! MAXWELL! HELP ME--

--PULL!

THEY ≈OOF≈ SAY "YOU CAN'T GO HOME AGAIN" FOR A ≈HFFF≈ *REASON,* MELODY.

WHAT WERE YOU *THINKING?* YOUR HOUSE *BURNED DOWN!*

WHERE DID YOU THINK THAT DOOR WAS GOING TO LEAD?

COULD YOU *PLEASE* KEEP IN MIND--

--THAT WE HAVE *NO IDEA* WHAT'S GOING ON--

--AND THAT YOU'RE *NOT EXACTLY* FILLING IN ANY BLANKS FOR US?

...POINT.

OKAY, YOU WANT ANSWERS? THIS IS A *THIRD EAR* AMULET. TALK *TO ME* THROUGH IT, WHEN YOU'RE OUT IN THE MUSEUM.

FIRST PLACE YOU'RE GOING IS--

WHOA!

TIME OUT! YOU THINK WE'RE GOING TO *DO* THIS FOR YOU?

YES, *OBVIOUSLY.* EVEN IF SOMEONE BESIDES YOU TWO *COULD* SAVE YOUR PARENTS--

--YOU SEE A LOT OF *VOLUNTEERS* AROUND?

SO WHY ARE WE PLAYING BY THE *KIDNAPPERS'* RULES?

EXPLAIN.

WHY DON'T WE GO *RESCUE* OUR PARENTS FROM THE--*WHOEVER* THEY ARE?

YOU CAN'T HURT THE *SHADOW SOCIETY.*

NOBODY CAN.

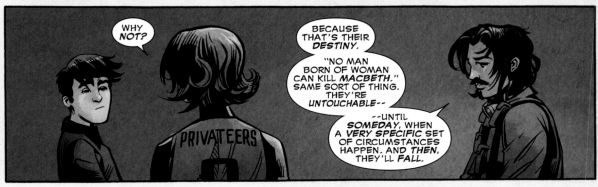

WHY *NOT?*

BECAUSE THAT'S THEIR *DESTINY.*

"NO MAN BORN OF WOMAN CAN KILL *MACBETH.*" SAME SORT OF THING. THEY'RE *UNTOUCHABLE*--

--UNTIL *SOMEDAY,* WHEN A *VERY SPECIFIC* SET OF CIRCUMSTANCES HAPPEN. AND *THEN,* THEY'LL *FALL.*

WHAT CIRCUMSTANCES ARE WE TALKING ABOUT, EXACTLY?

YOU'LL SEE.

POINT BEING--WE PLAY THE SOCIETY'S GAME. I TRAIN YOU TWO.

YOU DO WHAT NEEDS DOING. WE GET THE COFFIN CLOCK.

WE GET YOUR PARENTS BACK.

THIS SOUNDS LIKE A LOT OF...

...EXERCISE.

AND HOMEWORK.

YOU DON'T LIKE THIS? TOUGH.

I JUST LOST MY LEGS HELPING YOU. IT'S YOUR TURN TO MAKE SACRIFICES.

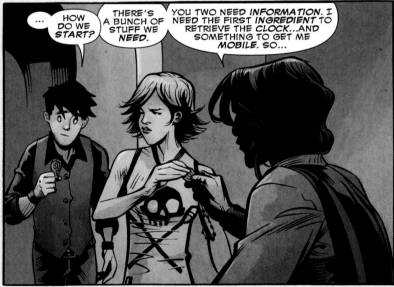

... HOW DO WE START?

THERE'S A BUNCH OF STUFF WE NEED.

YOU TWO NEED INFORMATION. I NEED THE FIRST INGREDIENT TO RETRIEVE THE CLOCK...AND SOMETHING TO GET ME MOBILE. SO...

...LET'S DO SOME ONE-STOP SHOPPING.

AND SO...

THIS IS THE WARDENS' LIBRARY. IT'S THE SAFEST--WELL, THE LEAST DANGEROUS-- PLACE IN THE MUSEUM, RIGHT NOW.

YOU'VE GOT QUESTIONS. THESE BOOKS? THEY'VE GOT ANSWERS.

I MEAN--

YOU DID MEAN HOMEWORK. BOO!

--IF YOU CATCH A BOOK AND ASK IT ONE QUESTION, IT'S FORCED TO ANSWER YOU.

SWEET!

WHAT DO YOU MEAN BY--

--CATCH?

OH.

GOTCHA!

NOW, WHAT DO I ASK IT?

ASK ABOUT THE MUSEUM!

OKAY...TELL ME ABOUT THIS *MUSEUM.* WHAT'S ITS *DEAL?*

HEAD-QUARTERS OF THE WARDENS--

--USED AS A *TRAINING INSTITUTION* AND A STOCKPILE OF *DANGEROUS SUPERNATURAL OBJECTS.*

WE'RE IN A *MAGICAL WEAPONS DEPOT?* WOW--

--*DARN!*

I CAUGHT *ANOTHER!*

OKAY--SO WHO ARE THE *"WARDENS"?*

GUARDIANS OF THE *WORLD'S FATE*--IN OLD ENGLISH, ITS *"WYRD."*

THEY COLLECT AND *PROTECT* SUPER-NATURAL DANGERS, KEEPING THEM FROM THOSE WHO WOULD *ABUSE THEM.*

HEY-- I *CAUGHT ONE!*

"*THOSE WHO WOULD ABUSE*" STUFF? LIKE THE *SHADOW SOCIETY,* RIGHT? TELL US ABOUT *THEM.*

THE WARDENS' *OPPOSITES,* THE SOCIETY HOARDS MAGICAL KNOWLEDGE FOR THEIR OWN SELFISH BENEFIT--

--AT THE EXPENSE OF THE *REST OF THE WORLD.*

COME TO *MAMA,* YOU LITTLE--

--*HA!*

IS THE *COFFIN CLOCK* ONE OF THE *DANGEROUS* THINGS YOU'RE TALKING ABOUT?

TELL US ABOUT THE *COFFIN--*

UH...

...*MELODY?*

...MAYBE I SHOULDN'T HAVE KNOCKED SO MANY OFF THE SHELVES...?

YEAH, NICE ONE, MAX.

UNCLE ROLAND? THE BOOKS ARE LOOKING, UH, ANGRY. WE'RE GOING TO GO.

⌐SIGH⌐ YOU CAN'T. NOT YET.

THE FIRST ARTIFACT I NEED TO SUMMON THE COFFIN CLOCK IS--

--THE ARMCHAIR WITH THE FACE ON IT.

WHY DIDN'T YOU TELL US THAT BEFORE WE CAME UP HERE?

BECAUSE ALL YOU WANT TO DO IS WASTE TIME GABBING, WHEN THERE'S WORK TO BE DONE!

OH, COME ON. LET'S NOT "WASTE" ANY MORE--

WHUD

OUCH!

VARLOT!

UM...THAT'S DIFFERENT?

WHAT IS? I CAN'T SEE! WHAT'S GOING ON?

MELODY! WHAT ARE YOU SEEING?

THE BOOKS ARE, LIKE--

--STACKING THEMSELVES? OR SOMETHING? MORE LIKE FORMING A HEAP?

EXECRATIONS.

LISTEN. GET OUT OF THERE QUICK--

--YOU'VE ANGERED THE LIBRARIAN!

THAT'S SUPPOSED TO BE A "LIBRARIAN"? WHAT'S IT--

MAXWELL! ON THREE--

--THREE!

WHOA, MELODY! DON'T DROP THE CHAIR--

WAIT-- YOU'RE CARRYING THE CHAIR?

IT'S A WALKING CHAIR, MAXWELL! IT'LL MOVE ITSELF FOR YOU--

WHAM

--JUST ASK IT!

NOW HE TELLS US?

COME ON, CHAIR-- --COME WITH ME!

YES, SIR.

THE LIBRARIAN ISN'T FOLLOWING.

WHY ISN'T IT FOLLOWING?

IT ONLY HAS POWER IN THE LIBRARY. DID YOU LEAVE?

UNCLE ROLAND, WE NEED TO GET YOU A "THIRD EYE," TOO.

OH, NO...

GREAT! JUST--

--GREAT?

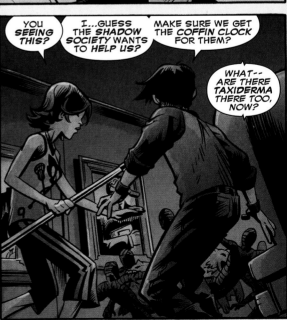

YOU SEEING THIS?

I...GUESS THE SHADOW SOCIETY WANTS TO HELP US?

MAKE SURE WE GET THE COFFIN CLOCK FOR THEM?

WHAT-- ARE THERE TAXIDERMA THERE TOO, NOW?

AND SO...

MUCH BETTER. CHAIR-- TAKE ME TO THE WARDENS' LIVING QUARTERS. DOUBLE-TIME.

YES, SIR.

WHAT'S THERE?

I TOLD YOU WHEN WE GOT HERE. BEDS. AND FOOD.

OH, GOOD! I'M STARVING!

ARE YOU A WARDEN, UNCLE ROLAND?

OBVIOUSLY.

AND OUR PARENTS?

AFTER THEIR FASHION. MUCH LESS SWASHBUCKLING THAN MY FASHION.

ARE THE WARDENS' LIVING QUARTERS GOING TO BE...

...SAFE?

YES--

"--ONCE WE MAKE THEM SAFE."

I THINK THAT'S THE LAST OF THE--UH-- "MUSHROOM PEOPLE." YOU'RE SURE THEY CAN'T HURT US?

THEY'RE JUST JANITORS. DON'T WORRY--

--UNLESS THEY COME AT YOU AS A GROUP. THEN, WORRY.

LOTS OF *SPACE* IN HERE. WHERE ARE THE *OTHER* WARDENS?

AND HOW COME MOM AND DAD NEVER LET US *MEET* YOU, UNCLE ROLAND?

LISTEN. I DON'T *ANSWER* QUESTIONS. I *ASK* THEM.

UNDERSTAND *THAT*-- AND WE'LL ALL BE *MORE* COMFORTABLE.

WOULD YOU *STOP* IT?

MAXWELL?

I'M TIRED OF YOUR *CRYPTIC JUNK!* WE'RE DOING WHAT YOU *TELL US,* ALL RIGHT?

STOP ACTING LIKE WE'RE *JERKS* FOR WANTING TO UNDERSTAND *WHAT'S GOING ON!*

THE CHAIR'S PART OF THE *"LIVING ROOM."* A SET OF *MAGICAL* FURNITURE. ASSEMBLE THE LIVING ROOM--

--IT SUMMONS THE *COFFIN CLOCK.*

WARDENS COLLECTED THE FURNITURE *YEARS* AGO-- BUT DIDN'T KNOW WHAT IT WAS *FOR...*

...UNTIL *THIS WEEK.*

WHEN MOM AND DAD FIGURED IT OUT...

...AND GOT *KIDNAPPED* FOR IT?

WE'VE GOT *ONE* PIECE OF THE LIVING ROOM--AND ARTHUR'S *NOTES.* SEVERAL *MORE* PIECES TO GO. WE'LL GET THE *NEXT* ONE...

"...IN THE MORNING."

YAWN IT'S ONLY BEEN **ONE DAY**...AND I ALREADY MISS HAVING **OTHER CLOTHES**.

I MISS MY **SHOWER**. DID YOU **LOOK** AT THAT CLAWFOOT TUB? WHAT KIND OF CLAWS **WERE** THOSE?

ENOUGH GROUSING.

WORK TO DO.

HOW 'BOUT THIS TIME YOU TELL US WHAT WE HAVE TO DO **BEFORE** WE HAVE TO DO IT?

YOU KIDS. SO UNADVENTUROUS.

I'M **PLENTY** ADVENTUROUS. I JUST DON'T LIKE--

KKKKKHHHHHRRRRKKK

--SURPRISES?

WHAT HAPPENED?

I **DON'T KNOW!** IT JUST STARTED MAKING **STRANGE** NOISES!

ROLAND? ARE YOU **THERE?**

UNCLE ROLAND?

I **THINK** WE SHOULD--

--GO MAKE SURE **ROLAND'S** OKAY. YEAH.

SOUNDS LIKE A **PLAN.**

WELL, NOW. YOU MUST BE **MAXWELL** AND **MELODY.**

ENCHANTED TO FINALLY MEET. WE'VE HEARD **SO** MUCH ABOUT YOU.

WHO ARE **YOU?**

ISN'T THAT **OBVIOUS?**

DISNEY KINGDOMS

SEEKERS OF THE WEIRD

COLLECT THEM ALL!

Set of 5 Hardcover Books ISBN: 978-1-61479-513-1

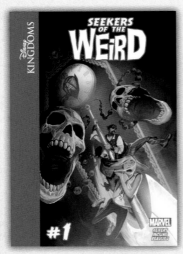

Hardcover Book ISBN
978-1-61479-514-8

Hardcover Book ISBN
978-1-61479-515-5

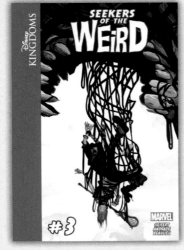

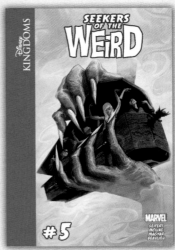

Hardcover Book ISBN
978-1-61479-516-2

Hardcover Book ISBN
978-1-61479-517-9

Hardcover Book ISBN
978-1-61479-518-6